P9-BAV-819

TWIST

To Julie Paschkis,
who has helped twist and shape my way of seeing
—J. W.

To Shannon McCall and Nan Yurkanis
—J. P.

Also by Janet S. Wong

Alex and the Wednesday Chess Club
Knock on Wood: Poems About Superstitions
Night Garden: Poems from the World of Dreams
You Have to Write
Grump
Behind the Wheel: Poems About Driving
The Rainbow Hand: Poems About Mothers and Children
Good Luck Gold and Other Poems
A Suitcase of Seaweed and Other Poems

Margaret K. McElderry Books

Margaret K. McElderry Books
An imprint of Simon & Schuster Children's Publishing Division
1230 Avenue of the Americas, New York, New York 10020
Text copyright © 2007 by Janet S. Wong
Illustrations copyright © 2007 by Julianne Paschkis
All rights reserved, including the right of reproduction in whole or in part in any form.
Book design by Sonia Chaghatzbanian
The text for this book is set in Syntax.
The illustrations for this book are rendered in watercolors.
Manufactured in China
2 4 6 8 10 9 7 5 3 1
Library of Congress Cataloging-in-Publication Data
Wong, Janet S.
Twist : yoga poems / written by Janet S. Wong ; illustrated by Julie Paschkis.
p. cm.
ISBN-13: 978-0-689-87394-2
ISBN-10: 0-689-87394-8
1. Yoga—Juvenile poetry. 2. Children's poetry, American. I. Paschkis, Julie. II. Title.
PS3573.O578T88 2007
811'.54—dc22
2005015888

TWIST
Yoga Poems

Written by Janet S. Wong
Illustrated by Julie Paschkis

WITHDRAWN

Fitchburg Public Library
5530 Lacy Road
Fitchburg, WI 53711

Margaret K. McElderry Books
NEW YORK LONDON TORONTO SYDNEY

CONTENTS

BREATH

Breath is a broom
sweeping your insides.

Smooth and slow:
You pull scattered bits of dream fluff
and heart dust into neat piles.

Short and quick:
You coax shards of broken thoughts
out of forgotten corners.

Breath is a broom
sweeping you fresh.

CHILD'S POSE

The chick-child curls up and breathes full.

Her body remembers the inside of the eggshell,
the firm roundness of her first home.

CAT/COW

Cat drops her head down to the grass.

Who would eat grass
when there is milk and cream?
Chills run up her hilly spine at the thought.

Wait: What if she could make her own milk?
She takes a nibble.

One bite:
And suddenly, magically, she turns into Cow.
She gazes at the heavens in gratitude,
her belly hanging low.

DOWN DOG

Down
is to dog

as up
is to bird.

Dog starts each morning
bow-wow-ing.

WARRIOR

A warrior

takes his stand,
feet planted sturdy and strong.

Before long, he sees
he is heading the wrong way.

He turns and

takes his stand,
feet planted sturdy and strong.

COBRA

Darkness
pushes Cobra up from damp soil.

She lifts herself higher,
to dry out her heart.

LOW CROW

Crow depends on his elbows.

You cannot always fly.
You need somewhere to rest
the weight of yourself.

HALF-MOON

One hot night

a girl stood in a field,
one leg out, one arm high,
and squawked,
Look, look at me—I can fly!

Grabbing hold of a star,
she became Half-Moon.

TRIANGLE

Head to foot to foot,
finger to finger to toe,
hand to ankle to hip:

My body is a puzzle of triangles.

The lines are invisible
but straight and strong.

TREE

Trees watch.

This is why
they grow tall,
this is why they bend
and sway,
so they can see around
a house, over a hill,
beyond a fire.

Look—not just on a windy day.
See how they move.
At the tip of each branch
there is an eye.

EAGLE

One foot toward the lake,
Eagle knows when fish wake up.

One foot toward the forest,
Eagle feels a squirrel jump.

Front and back twisted into back and front,
Eagle thinks here, and is there.

The whole meadow hushes
when Eagle raises her wing.

MOUNTAIN/ VOLCANO

I am Mountain.
My stillness is never still.

One hundred quakes:
now as I tuck my hips,
now as I roll my shoulders.

No:
I am Volcano,
pulsing
with the earth's energy
from my feet
up through my legs,
up through my spine.

My neck is soft with molten lava.
My arms are a spray of ash.
My breath is a stream of steam

rising—

whoosh!

LION

Tiredness
gets caught in your throat.

Lion casts it out with a fierce exhale,
mouth wide open,
and lets it roll off his tongue.

BRIDGE

A bridge is as good as its legs,
the pilings, the pillars that shoulder the weight
stretched tight in the middle,
floating.

FINDING THE CENTER

She reaches–
and she touches.

Knees to nose,
toes to neck.

She is the superyogi.
She is Scorpion,
she is Shooting Bow,
she is Frog,
she is Wheel.

I am doughnut.

Round jelly doughnut
with a sweet, soft center.

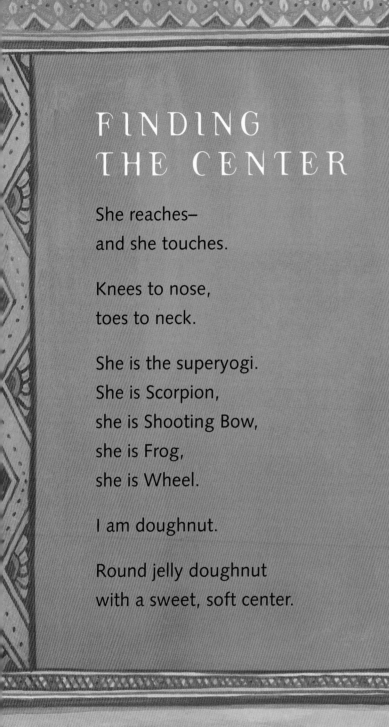

TWIST

I twist my legs left
and feel a pull in the right shoulder.

I twist right
and feel left.

I repeat your words to myself,
and now I hear what you said.

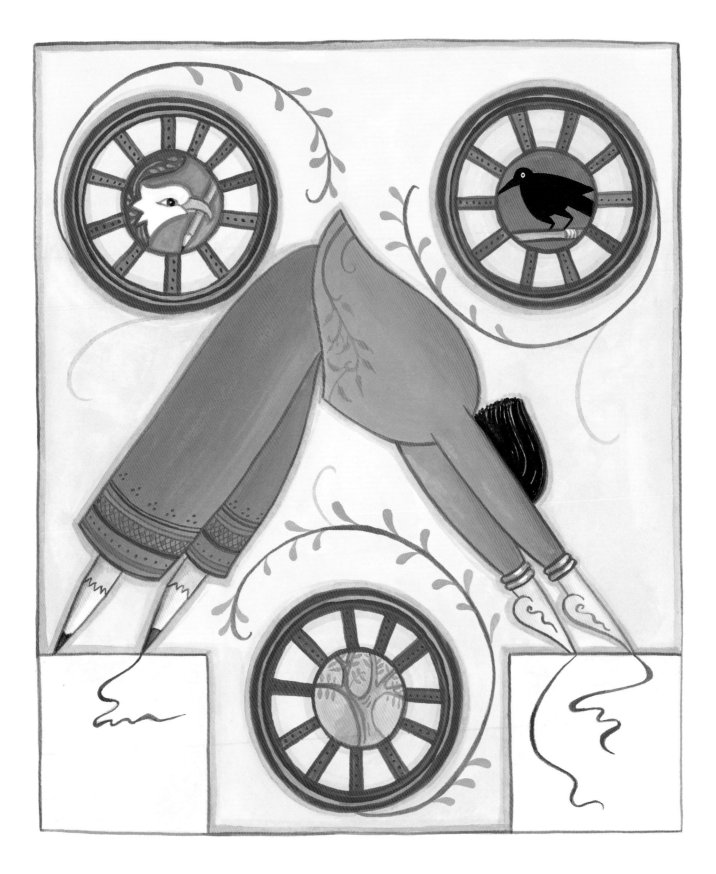

AUTHOR'S NOTE

I wrote these poems for Julie, the illustrator of this book. Julie loves yoga. Julie likes to stretch.

I like to stretch too, but I am wound up kind of tight. I hate it when I stretch but cannot reach. Some yoga people say it doesn't matter if you don't reach. You reach as far as you were meant to go.

I practiced yoga poses in my writing room while I wrote these poems. I would write a line, do the pose, jump up and write another line, and do the pose again, over and over. Sometimes I pushed myself a little too far. I looked at yoga pictures and forced my body to look somewhat the same way, even when it felt bad. Don't push yourself too far.

Writing about poses helped me understand them better. It also helped me have more fun while doing them. Suddenly I was not just in a twisted pose; I became Eagle, a hungry predator sensing every bit of movement around me. I became curious as a tree, sturdy as a bridge, worried as a crow. I became more comfortable with all the different things I am, especially my soft doughnut self.

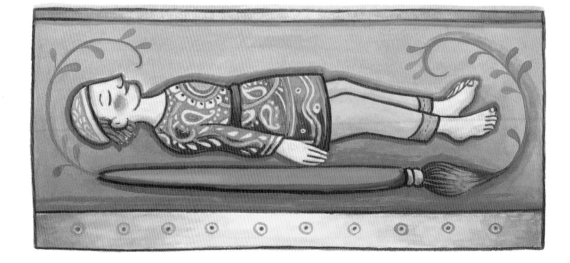